A WALK
IN
PARIS

Salvatore Rubbino

Place Maubert is in the Latin Quarter of Paris, south of the River Seine.

You can buy tickets for the métro at any station. Some shops and newspaper stands sell them as well.

Another name for Paris is the City of Light.

The métro is Paris's underground railway.

METRO

Maubert Mutualité

LE METRO DE PARIS

This *Paris* book belongs to:

_____

_____

WALKER BOOKS

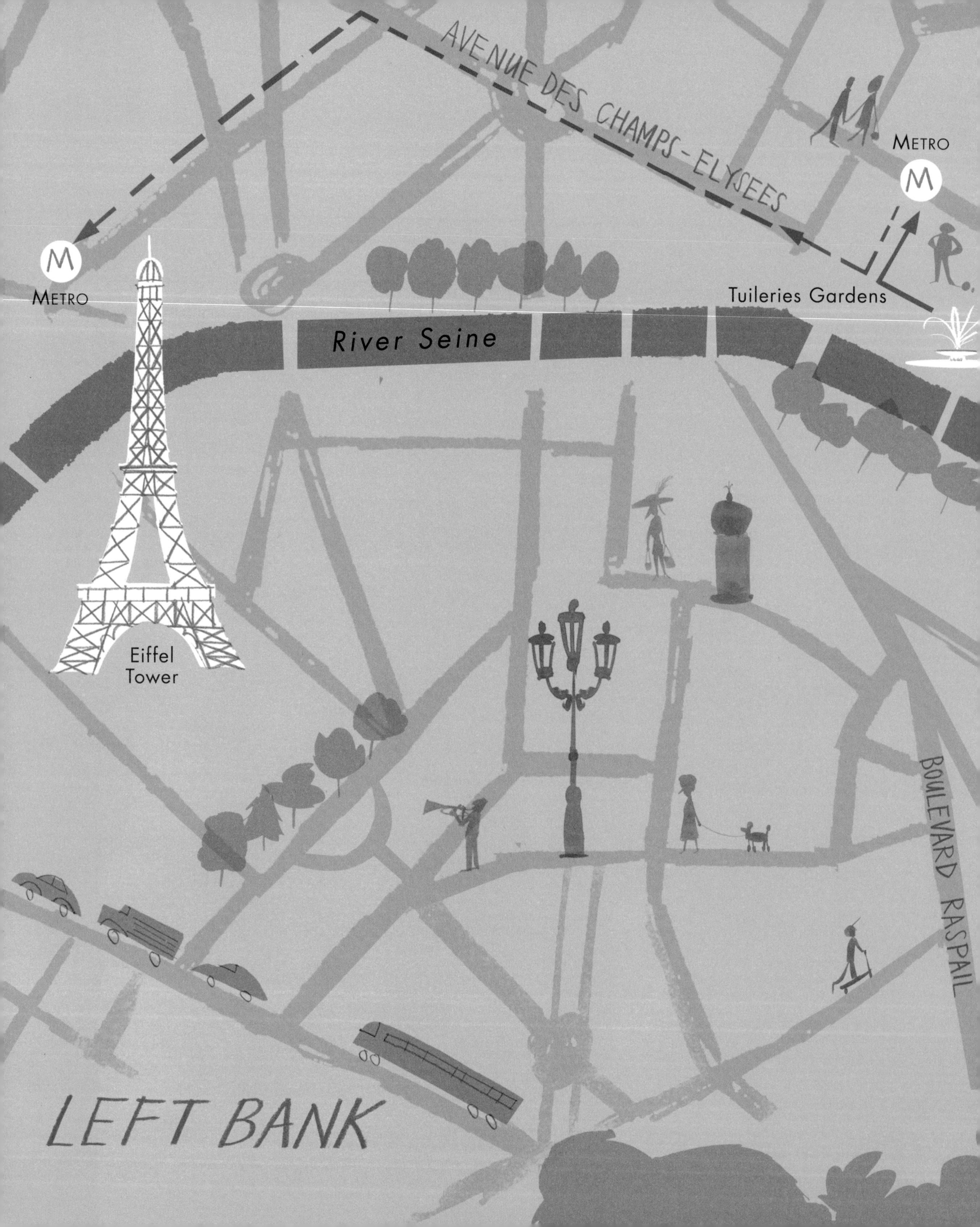

AVENUE DES CHAMPS-ELYSEES

METRO

METRO

Tuileries Gardens

River Seine

Eiffel
Tower

BOULEVARD RASPAIL

LEFT BANK

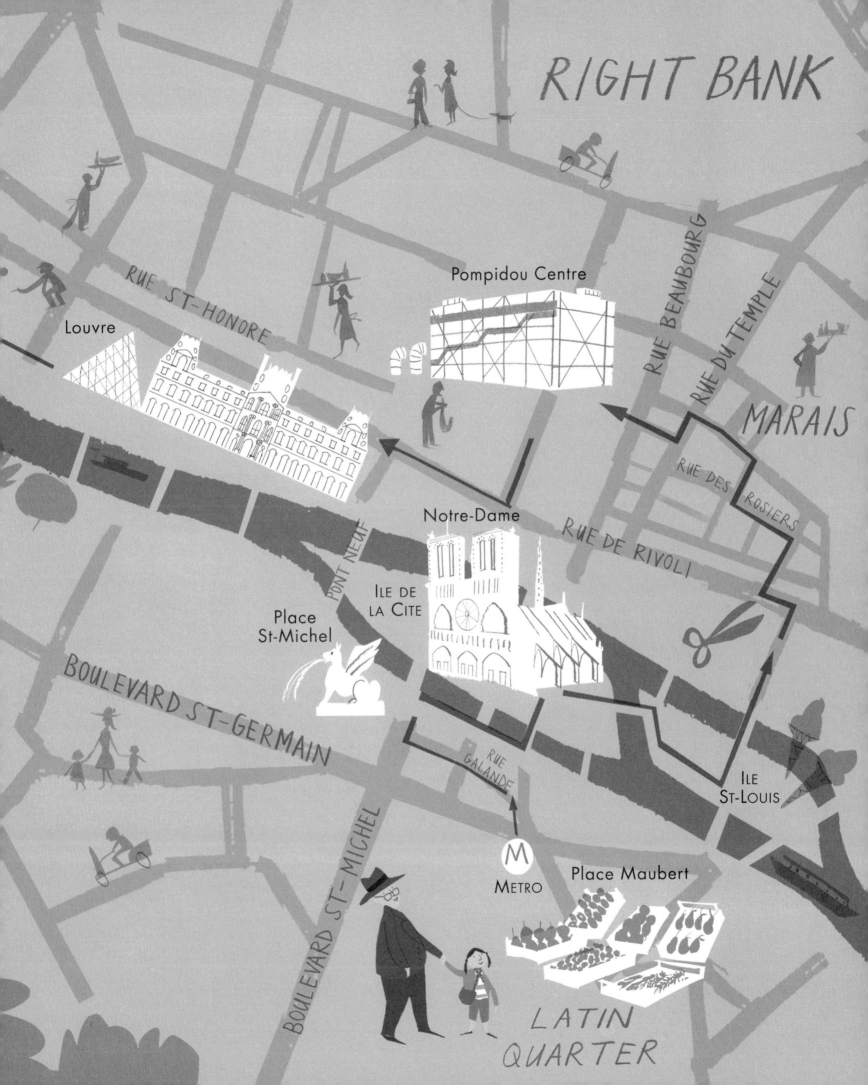

For Mum and Dad, Grazia and Vincenzo

First published 2014 by Walker Books Ltd, 87 Vauxhall Walk, London SE11 5HJ

This edition published 2015

4 6 8 10 9 7 5

© 2014 Salvatore Rubbino

The right of Salvatore Rubbino to be identified as author and illustrator of this work has been asserted by him in accordance with the Copyright, Designs and Patents Act 1988

This book has been typeset in MKlang Bold and Futura Book

Printed and bound in China

British Library Cataloguing in Publication Data: a catalogue record for this book is available from the British Library.

ISBN 978-1-4063-6006-6

www.walker.co.uk

WALKER BOOKS
AND SUBSIDIARIES
LONDON · BOSTON · SYDNEY · AUCKLAND

With special thanks to Billy Rubbino for the artwork on p.39

Hello! This is **me** and that's my grandad. We're in *Paris!*

Café METRO

We've just come up from the métro at Place Maubert!

I wonder what all those crates are for? "You'll see," promises Grandad with a smile.

7

Also a crab, s'il vous plaît.

Merci, Monsieur. Au revoir!

Stallholders at a market know a great deal about food and how to cook it.

Place Maubert is home to one of Paris's oldest street markets.

8

There are more than 400 cheeses in France, from the creamiest Brie to the smelliest Roquefort.

BRASSERIE

*Bonjour,
Madame!*

Merci!

They're full of fruit and vegetables!
It's market day in the square.

"Shoppers like to visit their favourite stalls," Grandad says,
"chatting and asking questions while they choose."

Mmm... I get some tasty cheese to try!

S'il vous plaît means Please,
Merci means Thank you,
Bonjour means Hello, and
Au revoir means Goodbye
in French.

Street markets are found all over Paris,
selling the freshest ingredients.
They open on different days, so if
you want to visit one you need
to check first!

We walk down a street where the houses lean together ...

The Emperor of France asked Baron Haussmann to rebuild Paris in the 19th century. Haussmann designed wide, straight boulevards, where all the roofs and balconies line up. He also improved Paris's water supply and sewage system, and created beautiful parks.

CREPES

VINS

Fruits de Mer

In medieval times, building stone was mined from under the city. Three hundred kilometres of underground tunnels remain!

to one where they stand apart!
"This kind of road is much newer,"
Grandad tells me. "It's called a boulevard."

It's really wide and busy. We'd better cross
quickly, before the lights change!

Meet you
at Place
St-Michel!

GRAND BAR

I've just seen a street-cleaner turn a big key.
Now there's water gushing out of the kerb!
"Mind your feet, Grandad!" I say.

"We have these special taps all over Paris,"
the other man explains. "They give us water
for cleaning, right on the street."

Wallace fountains like this one are a familiar
sight in Paris, positioned on busy pavements
and in squares. Throughout the summer,
they provide clean drinking water
to anyone who needs it.

Parisian street-cleaners wear
green uniforms and drive
green vans. Even their brooms
are green!

Paris has two water systems.
Water for drinking and water for
cleaning run through separate pipes.

The boulevard leads to a square where everyone stops!

"It's very well known," says Grandad.

The Latin Quarter has been a home to students since the Middle Ages. Paris's university, the old Sorbonne, was founded in this area and dates from the 13th century.

Good friends in France might exchange three or four kisses when they meet – or just shake hands.

Salut!

Bonjour!

Bonjour!

Salut!

Salut!

"People often meet their friends by the fountain at PLACE ST-MICHEL."

Place St-Michel stands at the heart of the Latin Quarter.

Salut is a more casual word for Hello.

SOUTH TOWER

You can climb up to the Chimera Gallery or the South Tower to see the view of Paris from Notre-Dame.

CHIMERA GALLERY

The cathedral's "great bell" – the biggest bell with the deepest sound – is called Emmanuel. It hangs in the South Tower belfry.

Napoleon crowned himself Emperor at Notre-Dame in 1804.

This island, Ile de la Cité, is the oldest part of the city. People first settled here more than 2000 years ago.

In French, the word queue means a tail, which is just what it looks like!

PARIS

Round a corner
we find the **RIVER SEINE!**

"What's that big church on the island?" I ask.

"The Cathedral of Notre-Dame," Grandad replies. "Would you
like to climb up and see the view?"

I would!

Bookstalls have lined
the river since the
mid-16th century.

We have to queue for quite a long time ...

but it's worth it!
It's lovely and breezy up here.

EIFFEL TOWER

LES INVALIDES

ARC DE TRIOMPHE

Thirty-seven bridges
cross the River Seine in Paris.
The oldest is Pont Neuf.

RIVER SEINE

These statues of beasts
are called chimeras.
They're made up
of body parts from
different creatures!

Notre-Dame's Chimera Gallery is 46 metres above the ground.

Grandad points out some landmarks. The tallest building we can see is called the Eiffel Tower.

SACRE-CŒUR

MONTMARTRE

SAINTE-CHAPELLE

SAINT JACQUES TOWER

LOUVRE

It took almost 200 years to build Notre-Dame.

The whole of Paris south of the river is called the Left Bank. North of the river, it's called the Right Bank.

We make our way back down to the ground

The bigger island is Ile de la Cité.

Visitors tour the river on big boats called Bateaux-Mouches.

The French flag is known as the *Tricolore*, which means "three colours" – blue, white and red.

BATEAUX-MOUCHES

and over another bridge.

Ile St-Louis is famous for its
ice-cream parlours.

"Paris has two
islands," Grandad
explains. "This is the
little one, Ile St-Louis."

We settle down close to
the water's edge. A boat
passes by, so I wave.
"Careful!" Grandad laughs.
"Don't fall in!"

We've crossed on to the Right Bank of the river. "Paris has *style*, don't you think?" Grandad asks as we pass a smart hairdresser's shop.

I think there are lots of ways to wear your hair!

Chic is another word for stylish.

21 COIFFEUR 21

Paris is a centre for fashion.
Haute couture clothes are made to measure
rather than bought in a shop.

The poodle is often thought
of as France's national dog.

No wonder I'm hungry. It's one o'clock!
We find a cosy **BISTRO** for our lunch.

BISTRO

Plats du Jour
entrées
Plats
Desserts

A *plat du jour* is the chef's special dish of the day.

Parisian waiters are highly trained professionals.

Steak-frites, or steak with French fries, is a popular bistro choice.

Most cafés and restaurants in Paris are happy to welcome dogs.

A bistro is a small restaurant, often family-run, that serves traditional food.

A brasserie also serves traditional food, but it is usually much bigger than a bistro.

Then we're ready to explore the *Marais*.

This is a GIANT doorway!

"It has to be wide enough for a horse and carriage," Grandad explains. "That's how people travelled years ago."

We turn down one street after another

Beigels & Pletzels

The Marais was once a marshland. Now it is a fashionable part of the city, full of shops, cafés and restaurants.

Chez Marianne

and I think
we might
be lost ...

← Place des VOSGES

Musée PICASSO

Musée CARNAVALET

Hôtel de SULLY

Centre POMPIDOU →

until Grandad points to
a strange-looking building.

"Here
we are.
Let's go
round the
front," he says.

"It's called the **POMPIDOU CENTRE**, and look! It has all its pipes and escalators on the outside."

I think it's *formidable!*

Formidable is French for wonderful.

The Pompidou Centre is a famous gallery for modern art.

Important parts of the building are colour-coded. Escalator shafts and lifts are painted red.

The architect's idea was to help people understand how a building works.

Sometimes artists work outside the Pompidou, drawing portraits on the pavement.

CAFE L'APRES-MIDI

Cafés are an important part of Paris life. They often have tables on the pavement.

We've walked a long way on a broad, busy road when we come to a window full of cakes!

"Which one would you like?" asks Grandad.

"Ummm... That one, that one, that one ... and

This kind of shop is a pâtisserie, a specialist bakery selling pastries and cakes.

Every tart, profiterole and éclair is created by a master pastry chef.

THAT one!"
I say.

The Mona Lisa is one of Leonardo da Vinci's best known paintings. Her eyes are said to follow you round the room.

Napoleon liked the picture so much that he hung it in his bedroom!

We turn into a courtyard with a pyramid in the middle!
And rows of tall, grand buildings round the sides.

The museum is housed in the buildings of an ancient palace.

MONA LISA

The main entrance to the Louvre is through the glass pyramid! Visitors take a lift or staircase down to a hall, then choose which building to enter from underground.

The pyramid, and the little pyramids nearby, are made of glass and steel. They were built in 1989.

A tour guide is talking to her group. "This is the LOUVRE MUSEUM," she says. "Its treasures include a famous painting called the Mona Lisa."

"I see the Mona Lisa!" I tell Grandad. "She's on that poster over there!"

31

We rest in the Tuileries Gardens.
Grandad enjoys his favourite view ...

The view is of the Triumphal Way, which is 9 km long and runs in a straight line through Paris.

Two important sites along the route are Place de la Concorde, with its obelisk, and the Arc de Triomphe.

while I make a friend by the water.

Boules is a classic French game. Each player tries to throw his *boule* as close as he can to the little one.

The first manned hydrogen balloon took off from the Tuileries Gardens in 1783. At least half the population of Paris turned out to watch.

Tile-making workshops (*tuileries*) occupied this piece of land until the mid-16th century, when it was turned into a formal garden by Catherine de Médicis.

METRO

Then Grandad says we need to find a métro station.

You can drag your chair wherever you want in the Tuileries Gardens.

Every spring and autumn the gardens are planted with up to 70,000 plants and bulbs.

The head gardener checks that all the flowering plants range between 70 cm and 1.2 m in height.

The trees in the Tuileries Gardens are trimmed regularly to keep the view clear.

SORTIE

PLACE DE LA CONCORDE
CÔTÉ JARDIN DES TUILERIES

The first métro line in Paris was opened in 1900.

The word *métro* is short for *métropolitain*.

Some of the métro trains have rubber wheels, which makes them feel bouncy inside.

Paris has the second busiest underground system in Europe, after Moscow.

016

101

We listen to a cheerful tune, waiting for our train.

"Where are we going?" I ask, but he won't tell me! "It's a surprise," he says.

PARFUM pour FEMME

TUILERI

Merci

Many métro lines in Paris follow the course of the streets above.

The sky's getting dark when we come up from the métro. Grandad buys me a souvenir from a kiosk by the station.

The word *souvenir* also means a memory in French.

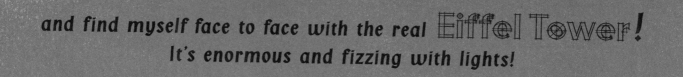

and find myself face to face with the real **Eiffel Tower**!
It's enormous and fizzing with lights!

A beacon of light sweeps across Paris from the top of the tower.

At 324 metres (including the antennae) the Eiffel Tower is the tallest building in Paris.

The Eiffel Tower sways a little in strong winds. It can also grow taller or shorter by up to 15 centimetres depending on the temperature.

The Eiffel Tower is bathed in golden light from dusk onwards. Then, for five minutes at the start of every hour, 20,000 extra lightbulbs sparkle on and off!

The Eiffel Tower was built by Gustave Eiffel and completed in 1889. The construction was a feat of engineering, taking only 2 years, 2 months and 5 days.

Double-decker lifts carry visitors to the top.

Since the 1960s the tower has been painted light brown to match its surroundings. Its earlier colours have included deep red and canary yellow.

The tower weighs 10,100 tons.

Many of Paris's monuments, churches, statues, fountains and bridges are lit up at night.

We stay till the end of the show.

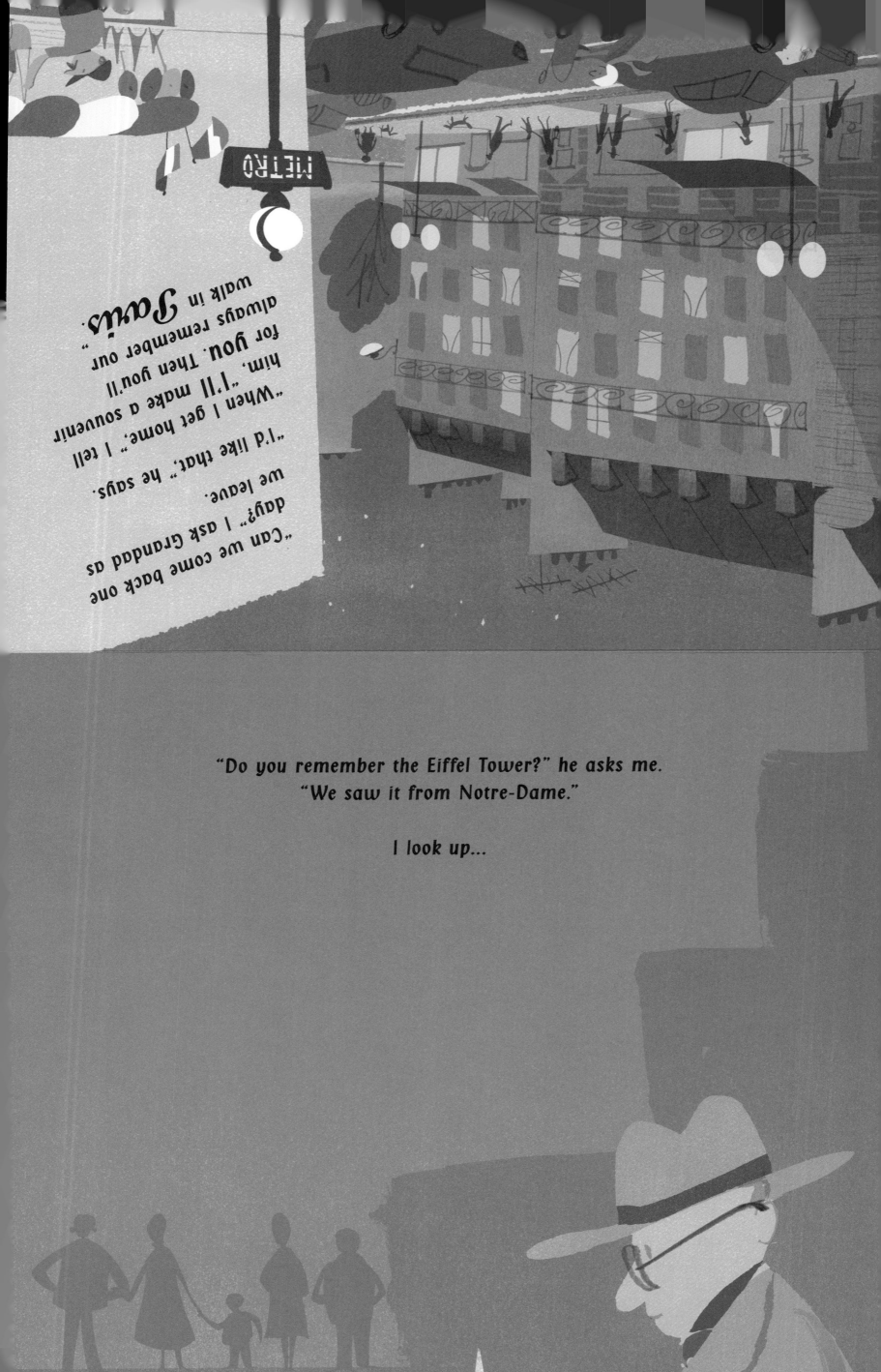

"Can we come back one day?" I ask Grandad as we leave.

"I'd like that," he says.

"When I get home," I tell him, "I'll make a souvenir for you. Then you'll always remember our walk in *Paris*."

"Do you remember the Eiffel Tower?" he asks me.
"We saw it from Notre-Dame."

I look up...

Merci
and au revoir!

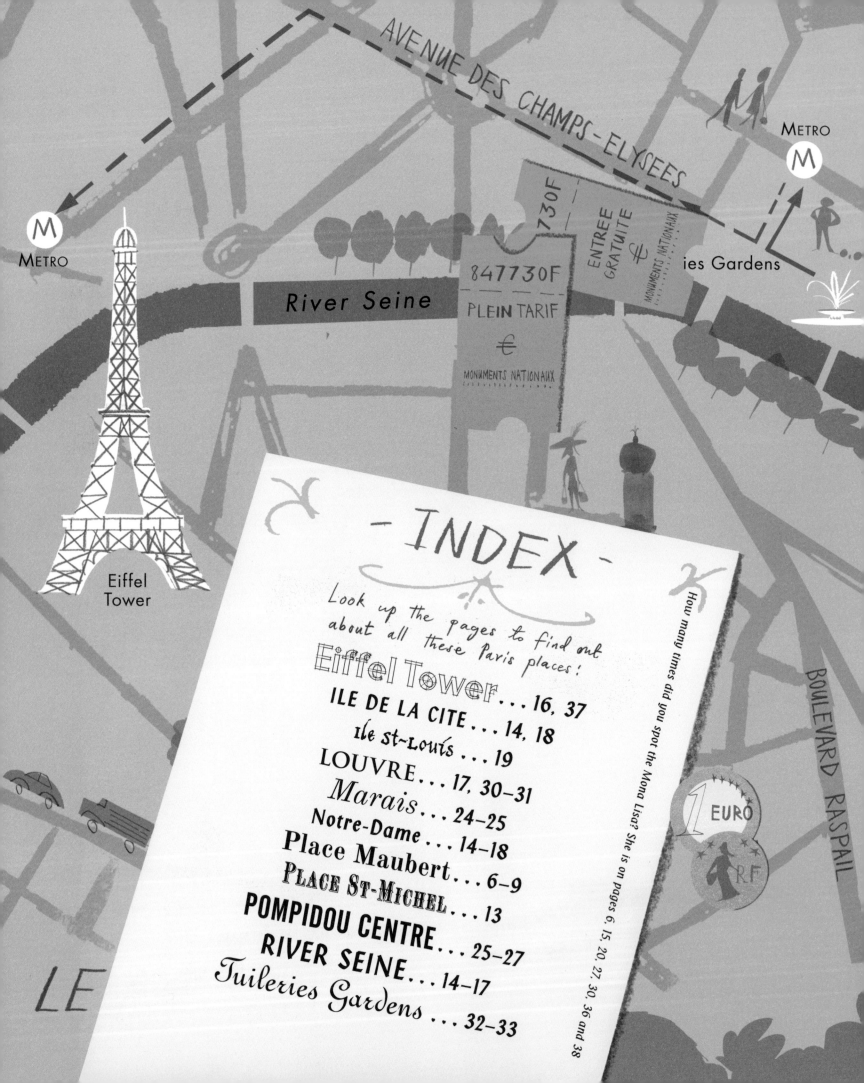

METRO M

AVENUE DES CHAMPS-ELYSEES

METRO M

730F

847730F

PLEIN TARIF
€
MONUMENTS NATIONAUX

ENTREE GRATUITE €
MONUMENTS NATIONAUX

River Seine

...ies Gardens

Eiffel Tower

BOULEVARD RASPAIL

LE

1 EURO
RF

How many times did you spot the Mona Lisa? She is on pages 6, 15, 20, 27, 30, 36 and 38

— INDEX —

Look up the pages to find out about all these Paris places:

Salvatore Rubbino loves walking and drawing in Paris.
When he gets tired, he likes to rest on the river bank with
an ice-cream, watching the boats go by.

If you enjoyed this book, why not take a walk around another city!

ISBN 978-1-4063-2180-7

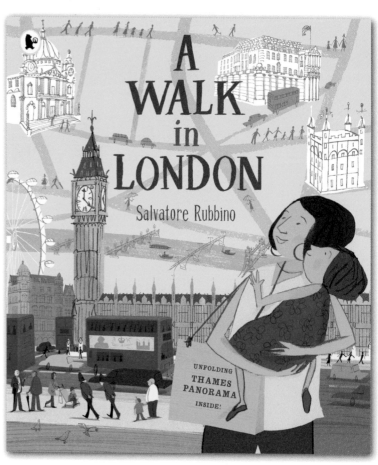

ISBN 978-1-4063-3779-2

Available from all good booksellers

www.walker.co.uk